JUST LIKE DAD
BY GINA AND MERCER MAYER

Westport, Connecticut

Published by Reader's Digest Young Families, Inc. Printed in the U.S.A. LITTLE CRITTER® is a registered trademark of
Mercer Mayer. READER'S DIGEST KIDS & DESIGN is a registered trademark of The Reader's Digest Association, Inc.
ISBN: 0-89577-768-1

When I grow up, I want to be just like my dad.

I'll be able to hit the baseball right
out of the ball park, just like Dad.
Well, at least I'll be able to hit it.

I'll have a big garden, just like Dad.
This is *my* garden.
Maybe I'll remember to water it
when I'm just like Dad.

I'll have a great job, just like Dad.
I'll have a briefcase, too. But I'll
play video games on my computer
all day long.

When I grow up, I'll be able
to drive a car, just like Dad.
Now he lets me sit on his lap
and pretend to drive.

I'll be a great cook, just like Dad.
He cooks lots of eggs.

I'll have my own money, just like Dad.
My dad says he hopes I have a lot more.

When I grow up, I'll be able to climb
a ladder to wash the windows,
just like Dad.
I won't even fall.

And I'll be able to build a fence,
just like Dad. I'll know how to use
a hammer and a screwdriver and
everything.

I'll be able to cut the grass with the tractor, just like Dad. He says he can't wait until I can do that.

When I grow up, I'll be able to
paint the shutters, just like Dad.
And I won't even get yelled at
when I make a mess.

I'll be able to watch anything I want on TV, just like Dad.
But I won't ever watch the news.

I'll take showers instead of baths, just like my dad. When I'm just like him, I won't want to play with my tub toys anymore. Maybe.

When I grow up, I'll be able to shave,
just like Dad. I'll be really careful
not to get cut.

And I'll wear cologne, just like Dad.
Then Mom will think I smell good, too.

I'll be able to go grocery shopping,
just like Dad. I'll buy anything I want.
I won't even have to ask.

And I'll eat a bowl of cereal every night
before bed, just like Dad.
Only I won't eat the kind he eats.

When I grow up, I'll be handsome,
just like Dad. He's the most handsome
critter in the whole world.